Gray Mountain: A Novel by John Grisham - Reviewed

By
J.T. Salrich

CONTENTS

About the author.. 8

Themes 9

Symbols 9

Settings 9

Chapter 1 12

Chapter 2 14

Chapter 3 16

Chapter 4 18

Chapter 5 20

Chapter 6 22

Chapter 7 24

Chapter 8 26

Chapter 9 29

Chapter 10 31

Chapter 11 33

Chapter 12 35

Chapter 13 37

Chapter 14 39

Chapter 15 41

Chapter 16 43

Chapter 17 45

Chapter 18 47

Chapter 19 49

Chapter 20 51

Chapter 21 53

Chapter 22 55

Chapter 23 57

Chapter 24 59

Chapter 25 61

Chapter 26 63

Chapter 27 65

Chapter 28 67

Chapter 29 69

Chapter 30 71

Chapter 31 73

Chapter 32 75

Chapter 33 77

Chapter 34 79

Chapter 35 81

Chapter 36 83

Chapter 37 85

Chapter 38 87

Chapter 39 89

Chapter 40 91

Critical Reviews 93

Final Thoughts 94

Glossary 95

Recommended Reading 99

About the author

John Grisham graduated from the University Of Mississippi School Of Law in 1981 and practiced criminal law for over a decade. While serving in the House of Representatives in Mississippi from January 1984 to September 1990, he began writing his first novel *A Time to kill* and published in June 1989.

This book was thought of after hearing a twelve year old on the stand recount her story of being beaten and raped to the jury. At the time Grisham was listening to her, he wondered what would have happened if her father had killed the men that had done that to her.

The story took Grisham three years to write and was rejected by twenty-eight publishers before Wynwood Press agreed to a 5000-copy printing. By this time Grisham was already working on his second novel *The Firm* that was published in 1991 and sold over seven million copies.

In 1993 the book was made into a film starring Tom Cruise. Since then, eight of Grisham's books have been made into movies. Grisham's books have sold over 275 million copies and have been translated into forty-two different languages.

Grisham shares honors with renowned authors Tom Clancy and J.K. Rowling for having sold over 2 million copies on first printing.

Themes

The major theme of this book is the plight of the coal miners. Many coal miners suffer terrible health problems including black lung disease. Although entitled to benefits from the hazards of working in the coalmines, man of the miners are too poor to fight the rich and powerful coal companies with their armies of lawyers.

This book notes the effects of the 2008 financial crisis on many big law firm lawyers, in addition, to highlighting the great work that non-profit legal aid provides to the working poor who cannot afford legal help.

Symbols

The main symbol for this book is "gray". The barrage of events and tragedies that surround Samantha constantly put her operating in a gray zone of the law. The book uses gray to point out that sometimes even the law is not so black and white. Grisham raises the interesting question of "Is operating in the gray zone legal and ethical even if done for moral reasons?"

Settings

Gray Mountain takes place in Brady, Virginia. This is a very small town in Appalachia country. The main character has ties with New York City and Washington, D.C so sometimes the story takes the reader to these places as well.

Short Summary

In *Gray Mountain*, a New York City lawyer, Samantha Kofer is placed on furlough from her law firm during the financial crisis of 2008. Instead of being fired she has the option to go work as an unpaid intern at an approved nonprofit firm for one year. If after one year, there is an opening, she will be allowed to return to the firm and keep her seniority.

Samantha accepts an internship at Mountain Legal Aid Clinic in Brady, Virginia run by Mattie Wyatt. Samantha befriends Donovan Gray who is Mattie's nephew and practically raised him and his brother Jeff. When Donovan's father got cheated out of his land sale to a coal company, Rose, Mattie's sister killed herself and Donovan's father ran off. Donovan became an attorney like his aunt and made it his sole purpose in life to sue the big coal companies and fight for the miners and their families.

Donovan tells Samantha that he has found some documents that are going to bring down one of the biggest coal mining companies in the country. After winning a major verdict in a black-lung disease, Donovan files his lawsuit and then is killed in a plane crash. Jeff, his brother, suspects foul play and brings Samantha in on his conspiracy theory. Samantha soon realizes that she is in a world that she never knew existed and is not sure she belongs. She is horrified to hear the stories of miners getting cheated out of needed money as they slowly and painfully die of black lung disease. She does not know what to make of people who lose their home because a debt-company can garnish their wages on a whim leaving them too little money to feed their children. Samantha is used to reading over documents about multi-billion dollar real estate deals, and now she has a client who, after being beaten by her husband, is facing jail time for him turning her into a meth addict.

Jeff suspects that Donovan was killed over the incriminating documents he had on Krull Mining, so he enlists Samantha's help to get the documents from the hiding place in Gray Mountain and deliver them to the new lawyer that is going to handle the case. The FBI begins to harass Samantha and the legal aid clinic but Samantha finally tells her mother at Justice what is going on and the FBI backs off.

Samantha waffles on what kind of life she wants, but after being touched by the lives of the working and dying poor in Brady, Virginia, she decides to stay and practice law where she is needed- and where she can make a difference.

Chapter 1

Samantha is an associate lawyer at one of the largest law firms, Scully & Pershing, in New York City. The setting is 2008 when the financial crisis hits and financial asset firm, Lehman Brothers, declares bankruptcy. As one of the major clients for Samantha's law firm, the folding of Lehman Brothers drastically affects the firm and, coupled with the financial crisis, many lawyers, from associates to partners, are being laid off.

On the twelfth day of the layoffs, Samantha and two other associates, Ben and Izabelle, are called into their boss's office. All three work for partner Andy Grubman in Commercial Real Estate. Andy walks them through the events that have led to the layoffs despite all the young lawyers knowing just as much as he does and what is coming. He recaps that Lehman Brothers has folded and the finance firm had funded three of their upcoming projects. Consequently, his department is being cut, and he must lay off his associates.

Andy tells them that even though some lawyers are just being on the spot terminated, Samantha, Ben and Izzie are being offered a furlough. All three will keep their health benefits if they intern at a qualified nonprofit for one year as determined by Human Resources. After one year, if possible, the firm will find a spot for them, and they will keep their seniority. Nothing is guaranteed.

The decision is immediate, and Samantha returns to her office space to find a lady waiting for her with a cardboard box. Samantha packs up all her belongings under the watchful eye of the firm's representative, Carmen. Izabelle meets up with Samantha after packing up her own things and they agree to meet up later for a drink.

On her way out, Samantha is in the elevator when Kirk Knight, senior partner in Mergers & Acquisitions and member of the executive committee, gets on the elevator. Knight is one of the major decision makers on who gets laid off and when and appears to be nervous and uncomfortable when he sees Samantha and Izabelle with their boxes. Knight gets off on floor 28, and Samantha wonders about this because the law firm floors leased 30 through 65. Samantha walks out of the building, sets her box down outside on the sidewalks and waits for a cab.

Analysis

This first chapter sets the stage for the storyline of the book: A furloughed lawyer goes to work at a nonprofit for one year while waiting out the financial crisis. The main character, Samantha is introduced, and there is a small glimpse at foreshadowing with the elevator scene in which Knight gets off on floor 28.

Study Questions

1) Why are so many layoffs being conducted at Scully & Pershing?

2) What specialty division did Samantha work for at the firm?

3) Why was it unusual for a partner to get off on floor 28?

4) What choice is Samantha given when called into her boss's office?

5) Who is laid off along with Samantha?

Important Terms

Lehman Brothers

Scully & Pershing

Furlough

Chapter 2

Samantha goes home to her SoHo loft and begins to think about the consequences of her being laid off from her job. She realizes that despite the loss of the $180,000 a year salary, she actually despised the job, the one hundred hour plus workweek, and feels a new sense of freedom. Feeling a little guilty about the amount of money her parents spent on her private education, Samantha thinks about a friend she knew who had a nervous breakdown after a year working at "big law" and retreated to a simple life in the mountains. Samantha admits to having felt envious of the simple lifestyle and continues to think about what she is going to do now.

Samantha calls her mother first, Karen Kofer, who is a senior attorney with the Department of Justice in Washington. Her mother sympathizes with Samantha's news and assures her that she will find another job. Samantha feels like her mother doesn't really understand the predicament she is in because her mother has job security. Samantha goes for a walk and then decides to call her father. Marshall Kofer was a high-powered attorney who sued airlines after crashes and made a fortune doing so. Samantha's parents divorced after Marshall was caught and confessed to a two-year affair with a paralegal. Eventually he was disbarred and spent three years in prison convicted of corruption after he opened up a series of shell companies throughout the Caribbean and Asia to hide his money.

Samantha's father listens empathetically to the news and offers to take her on a trip that she declines. He then offers Sally a job saying now she can practice "real law." Samantha continues to walk and think and passes a bar called Moke's Pub where she thinks of an old flame. Henry was an aspiring actor and they had dated for over a year, but eventually they broke up partly due to her work schedule and he went to L.A.

Samantha gets the list from HR of the approved nonprofits but hears that most of them are not taking on any attorneys - even for free. She tells her roommate, Blythe, she lost her job and Blythe, also an attorney, is worried that she is next as well. Samantha continues to lament the loss of her job and figure out how she really feels about it. She was always very driven to be a successful attorney, make the large salary and partner, but still can't decide if that's what she really wanted or that was just what was expected of her. While having drinks with Izabelle, Samantha says that she is thinking about not taking the furlough because she feels there has to be a better way to make a living and a better place to work then with the firm.

Analysis

The loss of her job with the firm causes Samantha to start and analyze her life. Was she really happy with her life? Is working big law the life that she wants? Samantha realizes that she feels a sense of freedom and has a chance to pursue something that will give her meaning and purpose in life. She sees what she does not want in her mother, the bureaucrat, and her father who was driven by money and power to corruption.

Study Questions

1) Why did Marshall Kofer go to prison?
2) Why does Samantha not feel like her mother understands her situation?
3) Why is Samantha almost feeling a sense of relief now over being laid off?
4) Why does Samantha feel a sense of guilt over being laid off?

Important Terms

Bureaucrat
Big Law
Shell Company

Chapter 3

After sleeping for twelve hours, Samantha wakes up the next morning ready to get out of the city. Realizing she hasn't been away in over seven weeks because of work, she packs and gets on a train for Washington, D.C. on the way there, she starts to send letters to the nonprofits that are on the HR list she was sent. One by one, she gets replies back that there are no vacancies but thanks for applying. Samantha can't believe that she can't even get a job as a volunteer.

Samantha meets with her father who offers her a job at his consulting firm made up of him and two other disbarred lawyers. Samantha is dubious as to what her father actually does but he explains that he and his partners consult for litigation funders and they make a lot of money doing this. Samantha declines the offer and Marshall leaves it as a standing offer should she change her mind. Samantha then leaves to have dinner with her mother and promising to have lunch with her father the next day.

While sitting at a coffee shop catching up on email, Samantha receives a message from a Mattie Wyatt at Mountain Legal Aid Clinic in Brady, Virginia. The message says that if she can talk right then to call her and a number is given. After being rejected by nine other nonprofits in one day, Samantha is inwardly relieved and thrilled to get this message and she punches in the number to her cell.

Analysis

Samantha is struggling to figure out what she needs to do. To help clear her head, she leaves the city and heads to D.C. to see her parents. Reality is starting to hit now, so she does decide to contact the nonprofits even though she had been leaning against the furlough. After receiving nine rejections, Samantha is more open than she probably would have been otherwise when contacted by Mattie Wyatt from Mountain Legal Aid.

Study Questions

1) What does Samantha decide to do the next morning after being laid off?

2) What does Marshall Kofer's firm do?

3) Why is Samantha relieved when she gets the message from Mattie Wyatt at Mountain Legal Aid?

4) Why does Samantha decline her father's offer?

Important terms

Litigation funders

Disbarred

Recession

Lobbyist

Chapter 4

Samantha calls the Mountain Legal Aid Clinic in Brady, Virginia. Mattie Wyatt founded the organization and has been the clinic's executive director for twenty-six years. Mattie tells Samantha that she has been getting numerous emails from rookie lawyers who are the same as her, and she will probably hire the first one who shows up to interview - provided that she like them. The clinic does not provide any criminal services but free legal aid for low-income clients for domestic relations, debt relief, housing, health care, education, and benefits due to black lung disease. In all, Mattie Wyatt, another attorney, a paralegal and receptionist, all women worked there. Samantha tells Mattie that she will be there the next day to interview.

Samantha has dinner with her mother and they continue to discuss the situation that Samantha is in. Samantha assures her mother that she is not going to work for her father despite the job offer and further discusses the furlough offer. Samantha's mother still thinks that she can find a paying job and does not really grasp the reality for big firm lawyers who are being laid off during the financial crisis. The subject is awkwardly changed to politics and Samantha decided that she would rent a car for the next few days and drive to Virginia.

Analysis

Samantha is continuing to have mixed feelings on what to do. After talking with Mattie Wyatt, she feels that the job is not really suited to her but she still feels a panic about what she is going to do. Even though she keeps saying that she really does not want to continue in big law or with the firm, Samantha continues to pursue the furlough. Samantha is realizing that the furlough is probably going to be her only option at this point during the financial crisis.

Study Questions

1) How long has Mattie Wyatt worked at Mountain Legal Aid in Brady, Virginia?

2) What are some of the cases that Mountain Legal Aid will help with?

3) Why does Samantha feel like her mother doesn't understand her predicament?

4) What does Samantha ultimately decide she is going to do?

Important Terms

Black lung disease

Mediation

Appalachia

Chapter 5

Samantha rents a car and heads out for Brady, Virginia. She calls her father, declines his job offer, and also avoids an email from Henry wanting to get together for a drink (Now that they are both unemployed maybe they could start things up again).

Crossing into Noland County, Virginia, Samantha is pulled over by an apparent police officer. She is informed by a rather strange talking and acting officer that she is under arrest for reckless driving as she was clocked at fifty-one in a twenty mile per hour zone. Samantha is informed that her car will be towed, and she is taken to the Brady jail. Once at the jail Donovan Gray who tells her that he is an attorney, her attorney, in fact and he has had all charges against her dismissed approaches her. Donovan tells Samantha that the man, Romney, who arrested her, is not really a police officer. He is the cousin of the sheriff with a long history of mental illness, and is generally just humored for when he arrests outsiders and brings them to jail.

After retrieving her car, Donovan and Samantha go to a café for a cup of coffee while they wait for Mattie to finish at court. Samantha notices that Donovan appears to be disliked by some of the patrons at the coffee shop, and she asks him about this. Donovan explains that he sues coal companies and this makes him unpopular among some residents who have different opinions about strip-mining. He then explains in some detail what strip mining is and the devastating effect it has in the long run to jobs, health, and the environment.

The conversation ends when Mattie calls Donovan to say that she is ready to meet Samantha.

Analysis

Samantha gets a new and nuanced look at small town life. From being arrested by a mentally ill family member of the sheriff to a long conversation about coal mining, Samantha is seeing a new world that is quite different than the one she is used to in New York City. Samantha seems simultaneously intrigued and confused, as she becomes the fish out of water.

Study Questions

1) Why is Samantha pulled over when entering Noland County?

2) What are some oddities about the police officer that should have raised a red flag for Samantha?

3) Whom does she meet at the jail and what is his relationship to Mattie Wyatt?

4) Why is strip-mining so damaging and dangerous to people and the environment?

Important terms

Hybrid

Strip-mining

Exxon *Valdez*

Chapter 6

Donovan and Samantha walk to Mountain Legal Aid Clinic and Samantha meets Mattie Wyatt. Mattie is not what Samantha expected in a lawyer with her died white hair and pink tips. Mattie asks Samantha about her work in New York, and Samantha tells her that she mostly did commercial real estate and building law. Samantha confesses to Mattie that she really did not enjoy her work very much, and like the clients even less. Mattie tells her that is quite the opposite in Brady where the clients are liked and appreciate the lawyers very much. Mattie says that between unemployment, meth and the coal companies, they stay quite busy at Mountain Legal Aid and need all the help that they can get. Mattie is interviewing another attorney in the morning, then the board, which essentially is her and Donovan, will meet and decide on whom they want to bring on board.

As the interview ends, Mattie insists that Samantha come over dinner telling her the roads are not safe this late and besides its basic Appalachian hospitality. Samantha hesitatingly agrees, and they walk a few blocks to Mattie's house. Chester Wyatt, Mattie's husband is in a rocking chair on the porch reading a newspaper when they arrive. After introductions, Chester goes inside to start cooking dinner and Mattie and Samantha enjoy some wine out on the porch. Mattie tells Samantha that Chester is a retired postal carrier, and that her father had worked his entire life in the coalmines dying at sixty-on from black lung disease.

The three enjoy a pleasant dinner and Samantha tells them a little more about herself including about her father whom they recall reading about in the news. The conversation ends up with talking about Big Law and the huge layoffs that are occurring because of the recession. After dinner, the three retire to the porch and Mattie tells Samantha more about Donovan. Donvan's family owned and lived on Gray Mountain, and when hard times hit the family, his father had sold the mountain and surrounding land to a strip-mining coal firm. The sale was supposed to be very profitable for the family, but the company ended up ruining the land and swindling the family out of most of the money owed to them. Donovan's father tried suing but he was no match for the financial resources and power of the big coal company. Their home became inhabitable and the water was polluted. Donovan's mother killed herself and his father ran off. Donovan then went to live with Chester and Mattie. After finishing law school, he had dedicated himself to fighting big coal companies.

Analysis

Samantha learns more about what kind of legal aid she will be doing. She is getting educated on coal companies and the process of strip-mining and the effects that has on people, both in terms of health and financially. Samantha likes Mattie, but is still not entirely comfortable with country hospitality and is trying to figure out if she fits into this kind of life, which is so different than the one that she is used to.

Study Questions

1) What is Samantha's initial impression of Mattie Wyatt?

2) What are the issues that keep Mountain Legal Aid Clinic busy?

3) What happened to Donovan's family?

4) Why does Donovan carry a gun?

Important Terms

Coal sludge

Geological survey

Chapter 7

Samantha is back in D.C and meets her father for dinner. On the way, she gets a call from Mattie who says that the board met and she is offered the job. Samantha accepts, and says that she will be there on Monday. Samantha tells her father about her adventure in Brady with Romney and her interview with Mattie. Marshall is unimpressed with a job that doesn't pay but does feel like Samantha has the chance to practice real law by suing companies. Samantha asks if he has ever sued a coal company, and he says no but he thinks one his partners did in the past. Marshall is unfamiliar with most of the issues with coal companies so Samantha fills him in and becomes upset when he appears to be checking out a younger woman that walks by. Marshall remains skeptical about the whole thing, but decides to support Samantha and comments that at least it is a long way from big law on Wall Street.

Samantha meets with Blythe the next day for lunch to discuss the future arrangements. Blythe thinks that she may be able to keep her job after all wants to stay in the apartment. Samantha agrees to pay her half for the next three months of the lease and feels like she will be back in New York by then. She then leaves to stay the night with her mother and rent a car. After consideration, Samantha decides to rent a car in Virginia so she will not have New York or New Jersey plates that would more than likely attract more unwanted attention from Romney in Brady.

Analysis

Samantha is warming up to the idea of interning at Mountain Legal Aid. She has already learned a lot about the coal companies and the issues surrounding them and is able to give her father a coherent narrative about what she has learned. Samantha is still unsure of what the future holds evidenced by her telling Blythe she feels she will probably be back in a few months. Still nervous about running in Romney again, Samantha rents a car and is ready to return to Brady.

Study Questions

1) What happens at the first restaurant where Samantha and her father meet to have dinner?

2) How does Marshall feel about Samantha interning at Mountain Aid Legal Clinic in Brady?

3) Why does Samantha get annoyed with her father during their meal?

4) Why does Samantha not lease a vehicle from New York City?

Important Terms

Slurry

Fannie Mae

Jihadists

Toxic waste

Earthen dams

Hillbilly

Chapter 8

Samantha has her first day at the legal aid clinic. She sits in on the first client of the day who is a middle aged woman named Lady Purvis. Lady's husband, Stocky, has been jailed for failing to pay a speeding ticket and an expired driver's license. The family had no money and were behind on mortgage payments for their trailer and a whole host of other bills and expenses.

The Purvis' two teenage children were threatening to leave home and look for work elsewhere to make a living. A firm called Judicial Response Associates (JRA) had been assigned to Stocky's case, which essentially is a debt-collecting firm that tacks on so many extra service fees that the original $175 bill was now totaling $400. As long as Stocky remained in jail the fees continued to accumulate and the Purvis' had very little chance of being able to pay their bills and keep their home. Mattie tells Lady that she will take their case and talk with JRA and the other collectors. A thankful and tearful Lady leaves the office and Samantha's next client arrives shortly after.

The second case Samantha sits in with is a domestic violence one. Annette Brevard, the junior partner, at the clinic takes it and again Samantha listens and takes notes. The thirty-six year old client, Phoebe, was viciously beaten again by her meth addict husband Randy. Although Phoebe does meth too, she claims to not be an addict. Samantha looks up the case and finds that Randy is charged with malicious wounding and is scheduled to be arraigned at 1:00pm. Phoebe is terrified that if Randy gets out of prison he will kill her for calling the police on him. Annette tells Phoebe that he will not kill her. The plan is made to file for divorce the next day and to request an injunction against him that will protect her. If Randy violates the injunction by going near Phoebe than he will go back to jail.

After Phoebe leaves, Samantha is I her office when Barb, the clinic secretary, tells her there is a client on the phone and she is the only one available. Samantha answers the phone and listens to a man, Joe Duncan, who has been denied Social Security disability benefits and is unable to work because of a back injury. Not really knowing what to do, Samantha tells him that she will review his case with their Social Security specialist and call him back.

At lunch all four, Mattie, Samantha, Annette and Barb eat together and discuss the morning cases. Samantha inquires about Joe Duncan, and Mattie tells her they do not handle any Social Security cases and he will be referred to another firm Cochrell and Rhoades. Samantha wonders why Barb forwarded the call to her since the legal aid clinic does not handle social security cases. Lunch ends with Mattie telling Samantha they are due in court in fifteen minutes.

Analysis

Samantha is feeling like a fish out of water as she begins her internship at the legal aid clinic. She is not used to having real people as her clients and doesn't know where to begin with the stories of hardship that she is hearing. Samantha is surprised that the cases are talked about freely at lunch, and is somewhat glad to be able to ask advice on what to do about her disability case. She is a little suspicious about why Barb sent her the call since the clinic does not handle those cases.

Study Questions

1) Why is Lady's husband in jail?

2) What is JRA and how are they making the situation worse for the Purvis's?

3) Why is Phoebe afraid for her life?

4) Why is Samantha surprised that everyone is talking about their cases at lunch?

Important terms

Injunction

Malicious wounding

Meth

Equal Protection Clause of the Fourteenth Amendment

Chapter 9

Samantha has her first day in the courtroom with Mountain Aid Legal Clinic. She is nervous because she has not had much experience in court other than the mock trials during law school, and, of course, when her father was on trial. Annette and Samantha meet with Richard, the prosecutor for Phoebe's case, and he feels that they will be able to keep Randy in jail while Phoebe has a chance to file the divorce, get and injunction and clear the area. Hump, Randy's lawyer, argues that if he stays in jail he will lose his job, but Phoebe tells the judge that her husband does not have a job other than temp work now and then and selling meth. The judge believes Phoebe over Randy's version of events given that she is the one with visible injuries and not him. Randy is ordered back to jail for a few days to continue to cool off.

Outside the courtroom, Annette, Samantha and Phoebe are met by two of Randy's meth friends who attempt to intimidate Phoebe into dropping thee charges. Samantha is a little rattled by this encounter but Annette assures her that thugs like these never mess with lawyers and she has nothing to worry about. Samantha is not so sure.

Samantha spends the evening having dinner with Annette and her two teenage children. She is living for free in Annette's garage that has an apartment overhead. Annette's two children, Kim, thirteen and Adam, ten are polite children who find Samantha interesting and enjoy spending time with her. After dinner, Samantha and Annette drink some wine and have some girl talk. Both admit to not really seeing anyone. Samantha because she was always too busy with work, and Annette because there is just slim pickings in a small town like Brady.

Samantha admits to Annette that she is not used to this kind of personal work where she is involved with people and their lives. Annette cautions her against getting too emotionally caught up in their drama, but admits that she has sleepless nights too over the tragedies and sad cases she has.

Analysis

Samantha has her first encounter in the courtroom, and is not too sure about how she feels dealing with real people and the problems they are having. She continues to feel a little overwhelmed and is trying to get her feet underneath for this new kind of law that she is practicing. Samantha is thankful for Annette helping her along and showing her the ropes. It seems like Annette is going to be a kind and patient mentor to Samantha.

Study Questions

1) What courtroom experience does Samantha have prior to her first day in court in Brady?

2) What is the outcome of the arraignment hearing for Phoebe's husband Stocky?

3) What happens immediately outside the courtroom when Phoebe walks out?

4) Why does Annette not date very much?

5) Why does Samantha feel a somewhat afraid of the work she is doing in Brady?

Important Terms

Debtor's prison

Garage apartment

Chapter 10

Donovan comes to the office the next day and invites Samantha to have lunch with him at his office. Samantha tries to spend a couple of hours studying in her office, but Barb asks her to come man the front while she steps out for a bit. Samantha is nervous about the phone ringing or someone coming in the door, and she has no idea about what to do or handle the situation. After referring another Social Security disability case to another firm, Mrs. Francine Crump comes in, an eighty-year-old woman who needs a will drafted.

Samantha takes her to a private room and talks to Mrs. Crump about what her wishes are for her will. Mrs. Crump states that she is in poor health and has five children that are scattered everywhere and really have nothing to do with her. She has over eighty acres in land that the coalmines have been trying to buy and she refuses. Adamant that her children get nothing, especially the land which her children will immediately sell to the coal companies, Mrs. Crump tells Samantha that she wants her will drafted so that her neighbor, Jolene, gets the land. The neighbors have a mutual agreement that whoever dies first gets their land. Samantha is unsure about how to draft this will knowing that such an agreement will surely by contested in court, so she asks Mrs. Crump to check back in a few days after Samantha has time to confer with her colleagues.

At lunchtime, Samantha goes over to Donovan's office, which she finds is in better shape and more tastefully decorated than the legal aid clinic. She notices a picture on a wall of a trailer of a trailer that is sheared in half by a large boulder that crashed into it. Donovan tells her that was one of his coal company cases where the boulder had been dislodged by the mining and rolled into the trailer killing two children that had been asleep inside. To Samantha's dismay she finds out that the lawsuit only offered $100,000 because as Donovan said dead kids in Appalachia are not worth much.

Donovan and Samantha share some chicken salad sandwiches for lunch and Donovan offers Samantha a job working for him as a research assistant. Samantha says that he will have to talk to Mattie, but she will think about it. She is not sure she wants to start working the massive hours again that she just left behind, but she tells him she will think about it. Samantha thinks about asking Donovan about his past thinking about what Mattie and Chester had told him about him, but decides another time. Donovan mysteriously says that he has had an interesting life and he will die young.

Analysis

Samantha has a new case and is unsure about what to about drafting Mrs. Crump's will. It seems like every day she is being reminded that she really just does not know how to practice this kind of law that Mountain Legal Aid offers. Donovan continues to educate her on his passion of suing the coal companies and explain why he does it. It seems that he is trying to draw her in to his specialty and the lunch at his office was an opportunity for her to see his pictures of coal company lawsuits and illustrate his point. There is ominous foreshadowing is offered at the end of the chapter by Donovan saying that he will die young.

Study Questions

1) Why does Donovan invite Samantha to lunch at his office?

2) Do you think that is right that $100,000 was offered for the killing of the two children in the trailer?

3) What is the main problem with Mrs. Crump not leaving any of her land and assets to her children?

4) What offer does Donovan make to Samantha?

5) What is meant by Donovan saying that he will die young?

Important terms

Punitive damages

Bar exam

Litigation

Chapter 11

Mattie takes Samantha for a drive through the mountains on the way to the courthouse. They stop briefly and Mattie points out three mountains that have been strip mined by coal companies. Samantha is shocked at the damage and devastation done to these mountains by the coalmines.

Once at the courthouse, Mattie confronts Laney Snowden who is the representative for JRA the debt firm that is tacking on fees to the Purvis case. Mattie offers a settlement of $300 total which Snowden declines. Mattie than threatens a lawsuit against the company and promises over two years of litigation and paperwork. Snowden is shocked and doesn't know what to say. Once before the judge, Stocky is released from jail and the grateful Purvis' leave the courthouse together.

That afternoon, Samantha and Annette are back in court for Phoebe's case against her husband Randy. Randy's lawyer insists it was just a fight as couple have and they should be able to work it out. Annette tells the judge that the divorce has been filed, the children are safe with relatives and furthermore they request the injunction so that Phoebe will be safe from her husband. Annette also tells the judge that she, Samantha and Phoebe were threatened by Randy's brother, Tony, and two of his friends outside the courthouse the other day. The judge grants the injunction and Randy has one hour with a deputy escort to retrieve some of his clothes and belongings from their home.

Samantha declines another dinner with Annette and her children ad settles into a quiet evening of reading the news. She scans an in-depth article about some ecoterrorists that have been sabotaging coal mine companies and shooting out the tires on their trucks. These are evidently experts as the shots are estimated to have come from over one thousand yards away and with 51-millimeter military style slugs. No one has been injured, and Samantha secretly feels support for these vigilantes attacking the coal companies. She thinks back briefly to her life in New York City and for a minute misses the nightlife there and a good martini, but the feeling doesn't last long and she reminds herself she can go back anytime.

Analysis

Samantha is getting quickly exposed to practicing law in the courthouse, and is starting to feel more comfortable with the process. She feels a sense of pride in having the opportunity to help people who so desperately need it and is warming up to this kind of practice. Samantha is getting drawn into the problems with the coal companies and is now doing extra reading in her free time about some of the cases and problems.

Study Questions

1) What is Samantha's reaction when she sees the mountains that have been strip-mined?

2) What does Mattie tell JRA will happen if they refuse her offer?

3) What is the judge's decision in Phoebe's case?

4) How much money does Mountain Legal Aid take in and where does the funding come from?

Important terms

Foundation money

Dummy lawsuit

Deadbeat

Chapter 12

Donavan takes Samantha on hike. He has a rifle with him, which he says is for protection against bears but Samantha is not too sure. They climb up the side of one of the mountains and find a spot to peer over the side to another ridge. Donovan continues to tell Samantha about strip mining and how the coal companies are destroying all the land around them as they sweep through mining their profits.

Donovan finally tells Samantha that they are actually trespassing on Strayhorn's land, the company that he is suing for causing the death of the two children in the trailer that was crushed by the boulder. They hike further up, and find a spot to settle and look. Samantha looks across with the binoculars Donovan hands her and she sees an enormous operation of trucks and bulldozers. Donovan tells her that in just two years they have razed off eight hundred feet of the mountain. Enid Mountain is expected to yield about three million tons of coal for the company at an average price of sixty dollars a ton.

Samantha sees the giant boulder that killed the two children, and they watch the miners as they prepare to start some blasting. They are startled from behind by a friend of Donovan, Vic, who introduces himself to Samantha as "friend of the mountain." Vic used to be a mine safety inspector but has now gone to the other side and testifies against coal companies. Vic is a lead witness for Donovan in the upcoming case. The three are spotted on the top of the ridge and know that it is time to go. They run back down the other side and Donovan and Samantha climb into the jeep and take off. Before long they run into a coal mining truck that tries to head them off, but Donovan's jeep is easily ably to go around it. After getting back to town, Donovan invites Samantha out for another adventure tomorrow, but without the guns and trespassing.

Analysis

Samantha sees for herself the environmental damage that the coal companies are doing to the land and she does not like it either. She is also beginning to suspect that there is more danger in what Donovan is trying to do in suing these big cola because she really doesn't believe that the rifle he brought was just for bears. She agrees to go on another outing with him the next day as long as there is no risk of being arrested for trespassing, run off the road, or shot.

Study Questions

1) What does Donovan take Samantha to see on the other side of the mountain?

2) Who sneaks up on Donovan and Samantha while they are spying on the coal mining operation?

3) Why is Donovan carrying a rifle with him?

4) What company is Donovan suing that caused the death of the two children in the trailer?

Important Terms

Mountain seams

Quaint

Discernible

Sassafras

Chapter 13

Blythe calls Samantha early Saturday morning, and is thrilled to tell her that she has not been laid off and looks like she is going to be able to keep her job after all. Samantha realizes that she feels a little homesick even though she has only been gone for two weeks even though it feels like much longer.

Samantha drives out to a small, seemingly abandoned airport to meet Donovan and to her surprise, she finds him working on a small Cessna 172 that is his plane. Somewhat nervous and even more hesitant, Samantha decides to go flying with him, and they take off. Donovan flies her over many big coal-mining sites over South Carolina, Virginia and Kentucky. Samantha cannot believe the vast extensive damage that the mining companies are doing to huge areas of mountains and land.

They fly back to West Virginia and circle over an area called Hammer Valley. Donovan tells her that Hammer Valley has the highest cancer rate in North America including liver, kidney, stomach and uterine cancer as well as leukemia. They fly over a huge earthen dam and view a large body of black liquid, which is the slurry pond. It is this sludge and poison that seeps into the ground and contaminates the water for the people that live in the area - and what is responsible for killing them.

Donovan lands the plane and he and Samantha meet Vic who is waiting for them. They then go to meet Jesse McKeever who Donovan is trying to recruit as a client for a massive lawsuit he is getting ready to file against Krull Mining creators of the slurry pond. Jesse lost his wife, one son, one daughter, one brother and two cousins to cancer. Vic had tested the water from the McKeever well and found that it was polluted with VOCs - volatile organic compounds. These are poisons that include vinyl chloride, trichloroethylene, mercury, lead and over a dozen others just as toxic. Jesse is not too sure that he wants to be a part of the lawsuit but he agrees to think it over.

Samantha questions Donovan about whether he can prove the company knew that they were contaminating the water supply for these people. Donovan says that there are internal documents stating quite clearly that the company knew that they were poisoning the water supply, but he is extremely elusive about answering about if he has these documents or if he does, how he acquired them.

Analysis

Samantha is becoming convinced that the coal mining companies are ruining the land and making the areas unsafe for people to live. She is not really sure if Donovan is being straight with her about how he is getting some of his information and why he really carries a rifle with him. Samantha insists that if she is going to work for him, he is going to have to be completely forthright with her. Off and on, Samantha is missing her life in New York and is wondering what she is getting herself involved with in Brady.

Study Questions

1) What news does Blythe have for Samantha?

2) What kind of cancers are happening in Hammer Valley because of the pollution?

3) How does Donovan say he can prove that Krull Mining knows they are poisoning the water?

Important Terms

Claustrophobic

Leukemia

Incriminating

Chapter 14

Donovan and Samantha are flying back and after a while, he lets her take the controls. He shows Samantha how to use the yoke to steer and raise and lower the plane. Samantha is scared and thrilled at the same time and before long realizes how easy flying seems to be, and becomes comfortable.

After Donovan takes a short nap while she is flying, he asks her where she would like to go. Samantha says that she would like to see Gray Mountain where he grew up. With a little hesitation, Donovan flies her over to his family's land and she sees the destruction of the land that is left from the coal mining company his father sold to. Donovan points out a small white cross next to a creek and says that is where he found his mother. Samantha realizes that Mattie left out that Donovan was the one who found his mother when she killed herself.

Donovan takes Samantha back to the airport and then says goodbye telling her that he is off to see his wife and daughter in Roanoke. Samantha has dinner over at Mattie and Chester's along with Claudelle, their paralegal, Annette and her two children. Samantha is puzzled over a new and strange coolness that Annette has towards her and begins to suspect that it has something to do with Donovan.

Analysis

Samantha is beginning to think about how close she and Donovan are getting. She reminds herself that she really doesn't know what the status is with his marriage and she needs to probably watch the lines. This is re-emphasized when he leaves her to go see his wife and daughter, and by the strange way that Annette is acting around her now.

Study Questions

1) What does Donovan let Samantha do for the first time in her life?

2) What does Donavan point out to Samantha while they are flying?

3) Who does Donovan leave Samantha to go see?

Important terms

Detached coolness

Yoke

Altimeter

Paralegal

Chapter 15

On Sunday morning church bells, awaken Samantha and she realizes that she has slept again for a wonderful nine hours. She calls her mother who talks about the stresses and problems she has with cases at Justice and makes an insincere offer to come to Brady and visit Samantha.

Wanting to avoid Annette and the kids, Samantha grabs a map, cup of coffee and heads out for a long drive. She passes many packed churches and wonders about all the different kind of Baptists there are and the differences: Missionary, Southern, General, Primitive etc. Along the road she sees coal truck, coal signs and mines and she is determined to try and have a break from thinking about all the coal-mining issues today.

She makes it to Charleston but is uncomfortable with the traffic, so grabs a quick bite to eat and heads back to Brady. She goes to the office around 9pm and after an hour of reading calls Donovan. He is working late in his office prepping for a trial that starts the next day and asks her to come over and meet someone. Donovan introduces her to Lenny Charlton who is a paid jury consultant. Samantha does not know how she feels about prying through the private lives of potential jurors and is reminded again of how she really does not like the courtroom. Samantha then asks Donovan point blank if he has the documents from Krull Mining that indicate they knew about the poisoned water. She is adamant that she know the truth if she is going to work for him. Donovan appears to get angry but he simply pleads the fifth, and Samantha then says that she declines his job offer. Donovan somewhat coldly shrugs it off, and says that's fine and he has work to do.

Back at the office, Samantha reads a long brief in the back of a binder that tells the story of a miner with a family who died a slow painful death from black lung disease. At the end she realizes that the story is about Mattie's father.

Analysis

Samantha is already growing weary of the enormous problems and implications of big coal and what the strip mining is doing to both people and the environment. She is also growing a little wary of Donovan and is not sure that she can entirely trust him. Going with her gut until she finds out more of the truth, Samantha declines the job working for Donovan as his research assistant.

Study Questions

1) What does Samantha decide to do for the day?

2) Who does Donovan introduce Samantha to whom she does not like?

3) What does Samantha discover back at the office and who is it about?

Important Terms

Different kinds of Baptists

Jury consultant

David and Goliath

Coal worker's pneumoconiosis (CWP)

Fibrosis

Chapter 16

Samantha begins her day at Mountain Legal Aid Clinic with a destitute mother that comes in crying with her two children in tow. Pamela Booker, and her children Trevor, seven, and Mandy, eleven, had lost their home and had been living in her car for over two days. Pamela said that she had been working at a factory making lamps, but when a debt-collecting agency began garnishing her wages for a decade old credit card debt, she had been fired. The boss said that wage garnishment was just too much hassle for the bookkeeper. To add to the damage, the garnishment did not leave the single mother enough money for rent and food, so they were now homeless and hungry. Samantha is deeply grieved by this story and sends out for food for the family, and talks to Annette about what to do. She calls the boss and offers a subtle threat of lawsuit if he doesn't reconsider, and then researches the old debt. She finds that the court order was expired and so files a lawsuit against the debt-collecting agency for damages. Samantha is feeling pretty proud of herself for filing her first lawsuit, and agrees with Mattie that probably for the first time, she feels like a lawyer.

The drama continues when Randy and Phoebe Fanning arrive at the office to say that they have made up and Phoebe wants to drop the divorce. She states that she loves Randy and it was all just a fight and misunderstanding and she does not know what she would do without him. Annette is furious and reminds Randy that he is still under a restraining order, which he is now violating, but he insists that his lawyer is getting that dropped. They also want the malicious wounding charges dropped but Annette advises them that is up to the State and unlikely to happen given the statements and evidence.

Mrs. Francine Crump then comes in to sign her will that she had asked Samantha to draft. Tears flow down the old ladies cheeks as she tells Samantha that her beloved neighbors that she had trusted to take care of her land had sold out to the coal companies and were moving to Florida. Mrs. Crump doesn't know what to do now and leaves the office with the will unsigned.

After filing the debt lawsuit at the courthouse, Samantha stops in at the courtroom where Donovan is beginning his case. She arrives just as the judge is giving his instructions to the jury. After watching Donovan engage with the jury for a few minutes, she leaves and head home. On the way, she notices a whit pickup truck run up very closely behind her. It follows her for a while and then turns away.

Analysis

Samantha is getting exposed to and educated in a kind of law that she has never know or practiced. She is slowly becoming drawn into the reward of helping people that truly need it, and there is a passion for this kind of work that is building within her. Although she seems to feel more like a social worker than a lawyer, she is also learning that being a lawyer can be more than just writing and reviewing contracts for the insanely rich. Something is wrong though, and she can't quite figure it out. She continues to get a cool vibe from Annette, and something was definitely strange with her being followed by the white pickup truck.

Study Questions

1) Why did Pamela lose her job?

2) What is wage garnishment?

3) Why did Phoebe drop the divorce decree against her husband?

4) Why does Samantha feel more like a social worker than a lawyer?

Important Terms

Devour

Bottom feeding collection agency

Credit card judgment

Wage garnishment

Unencumbered

Hot-sheets joint

Chapter 17

Samantha takes a pizza over to Pamela and her children that the clinic has put up in a motel in lieu of remaining in their car. She had stopped by the school and talked to the principal and picked up the kids homework so they could stay somewhat on track.

Shortly after arriving home, Annette calls her and asks her to stop in for dinner. Samantha is a little weary of not having much alone time, but she also decides she wants to clear the air with Annette and find out what the problem is. After a casual recap of the day and the various clients and drama, the real discussion begins. As Samantha had suspected, Annette has a problem with the amount of time she has been spending with Donovan and especially the attention that Donovan has been showing Samantha. Annette reminds Samantha that Donovan is a married man and a ladies man as well. She tries to suggest that Donovan probably has an open relationship with his wife. Samantha concludes that Annette is jealous of her and is having an affair with Donovan herself. Now Annette feels cast aside because Samantha is the new girl in town and has captured Donovan's attention. Samantha is even gladder now that she refused to take the job working for Donovan because she admits she probably would have ended up sleeping with him as well.

Analysis

The air is finally cleared between Annette and Samantha and as was kind of obvious, the fact is that Annette is jealous of the time and attention Donovan is showing Samantha. It seems obvious that Annette is having a fling with Donovan and is not taking it well at being cast aside for Samantha. Samantha has made a decision that she probably needs to watch herself around Donovan because thought he is cute and sexy, he really is nothing but trouble and she just does not need that right now.

Study Questions

1) Who does Samantha take dinner to after work?

2) Why does Annette ask Samantha to come over and talk?

3) Why was Annette being somewhat cold and aloof to Samantha the last couple of days?

4) Do you think Donovan genuinely likes Samantha or is just maintaining his reputation as a ladies man?

Important Terms

Brick oven pizza

Strip mall

Kinfolk

Tight as a tick

Open marriage

Chapter 18

Samantha meets with Pamela's boss at the lamp factory. He promises to giver Pamela back her job if Samantha can win the lawsuit and stop the garnishment. Without really being sure of any time frame, Samantha tells him that the case should be resolved in a week. He then tries to retain Samantha but she tells him that she only works for poor people in need and leaves.

Life in Brady at the end of the workday is very different then what she is used to in New York. In the city she would head to the nearest bar or nightlife spot and hustle with potential clients and talk about the cases with other scrambling attorneys like herself. In Brady there a couple of seedy bars that do not really appeal to her and no nightlife to speak of. Samantha and Mattie have settled in to a new routine of talking about the day over a diet coke, and that is the most excitement Samantha seems to be getting at the end of the workday.

On this day, Mattie forgot to lock the door and they ended up have two clients walk in after hours. Buddy and Mavis Ryzer need legal help fighting the coal company over Buddy's severe case of black lung disease. He has worked as a surface miner for years and has one the worst kinds of black lung disease known as "complicated coal worker's pneumoconiosis." Although he is entitled to monthly payments of $939, the coal company hired a law firm, Casper Slate, who was able to get the judgment reversed with an army of their own doctors that said Buddy's trouble breathing was from a spot on his lungs and not from coal dust. Mattie is very familiar with this law firm and tells Samantha they are vicious, powerful and very good at what they do.

Mattie tells Samantha that she needs to think long and hard about if she wants to start getting involved in black lung cases. She reminds Samantha that these cases can rage on for years and years. Samantha is just "passing by" as Mattie says and the cases will be left on her desk when she leaves - cases that involve people that are hoping for help. Samantha grabs a sandwich at the local grill after Mattie leaves, and then heads back to the office to start going through the bags of paperwork left by the Ryzer's.

Analysis

Samantha hears her first black lung case and is moved by the story. She understands what Mattie is saying that these cases are hard to fight and very lengthy, but she can't help feel like she should do something to help these people. As Samantha decides to go back to the office and start going through the paperwork, it seems that she is changing and maybe going to turn into a different kind of lawyer after all.

Study Questions

1) What agreement does Samantha reach with Pamela's boss at the lamp factory?

2) Why does Samantha say she will not work for Mr. Simmons?

3) Why are the Ryzer's not getting the monthly black lung payments ordered by the judge?

4) How long can a black lung case take to be settled in court?

5) Why does Samantha go back to the office after getting some dinner?

Important Terms

Pneumoconiosis

Benign

Chapter 19

Samantha drives to Beckley, West Virginia to retrieve medical records for Buddy Ryzer. Among the files she finds documents that show that the coal company Casper Slate knew about Buddy's black lung disease years before he filed for claims and they buried the evidence. Samantha asks Mattie how they can do that and Mattie explains the differences between hearings and trials. In hearings, the same full disclosure is not required as it is in trials. Samantha is frustrated over the apparent fraud on the part of the coal company and their lawyers and wants to sue in federal court. Mattie explains the beginning steps but warns Samantha that the fight is hard, long and less than five percent ever really win. Mattie also suggests that Samantha talk to Donovan about it because he has more experience with going after the big coal companies and their lawyers.

Mattie and Samantha then head over to Donovan's office where he is celebrating the end of his case of which he is feeling very good about. He turned down a last minute settlement offer of half a million for the death of the two boys. Mattie, Samantha and Vic all tell Donovan he should take the money but Donovan is adamant that he can get more. Donovan practices his closing arguments on his audience, and Samantha is impressed with the graciousness and style in which he moves and speaks.

Samantha then heads over to the motel where the clinic has put up Pamela and her children to check on them. Pamela thinks that she may have found an apartment for four hundred a month and Samantha agrees to drive her there the next day to take a look.

Analysis

Samantha begins to look into Buddy Ryzer's case and is astonished at the fraud she finds that has robbed this man and his family of money he is entitled to her. She seems almost naively shocked that lawyers would knowingly deceive like that and become righteously indignant towards them. Samantha continues to grow and develop into a new kind of lawyer and is becoming less and less of the big city real estate lawyer that she was.

Study Questions

1) What does Samantha find in Buddy's medical files?

2) Why does Mattie caution Samantha against suing the lawyers for fraud?

3) What does Donovan give Samantha to drink that she has never tried before?

4) How much money is Donovan asking the jury for in the death of the two boys?

5) Why does everyone think Donovan should take the half million-dollar settlement offer?

Important Terms

Settlement offer

Hyperbole

Slew

Unethical conduct

Pathologist

Chapter 20

Samantha picks up Pamela and they spend most of the day looking at places for Pamela and her children to live in. Pamela settles on a trailer and Mattie says the clinic will pay the first three months of $500 rent. After that, Pamela will have to make ends meet herself. Samantha has not heard anything back about the lawsuit she has filed for Pamela, but she talks to her boss again who says he will take her back when the wage garnishment is over.

Mrs. Francine Crump returns to sign her will and is very sad and tearful about the whole affair. She has decided to leave her land to a company called Mountain Trust that vows to preserve land and protect it from the coal companies.

Most of the day is spent waiting on the big verdict from Donovan's trial. Right before jury deliberations the defendants upped their offer to $900,000 but Donovan still refused. After a painstaking few hours wait, the jury returns with a three million dollar verdict, an amount unheard of in that part of the country and Donovan's largest. Everyone celebrates and heads over to Mattie's for burgers on the grill, beer and champagne.

Analysis

Samantha continues to help Pamela and feels that being a social worker is also part of her life now as well as being a lawyer. She also is getting drawn into and attracted by the thrill and drama of litigation and begins to wonder if she could be a trial lawyer. Samantha feels like she understands her father better as she tasted some of the adrenalin rush of waiting for Donovan's trial verdict and then reveling in the astounding victory.

Study Questions

1) How is Pamela going to pay for rent at her new trailer?

2) Why is Mrs. Crump so sad about signing her will?

3) What last minute offer does Donovan turn down from the defendant?

4) How much does the jury award Lisa for the death of her two boys?

5) Why is three million dollars not very much for the coal company?

Important Terms

Insufferable

Legally competent

Family brawl

Overdose of testosterone

Chapter 21

Samantha, Donovan and Jeff fly to Virginia to talk with Marshall Kofer, Samantha's father. Donovan is interested in Samantha's case with Buddy Ryzer and he asks Marshall about how using litigation funders works. Marshall explains that the investors will put up he funds for the cost of the litigation for a take of the verdict. Marshall acts as the broker between the two and after reading the notes on the case, he feels very comfortable recommending to his investors that they put up the one or two million dollars needed to pursue the case. Marshall then asks Donovan about the Hammer Valley cancer cluster case, but Donovan evades the questions and Samantha indicates that she had not talked to her father about it.

Later the four head to a sports bar to eat and talk some more. Samantha mostly listens and is sort of turned off by the ruthlessness of it all and the brazen talk of just how much money can be made. Now she thinks that maybe litigation isn't for her if it really this cold and harsh.

Analysis

Samantha leads Donovan to her father to see if they can secure funding to begin the case for Buddy Ryzer. Samantha is dismayed at even though the evidence is there, it will take so much time and money to fight that they don't have. She realizes that she is stepping into her father's world with this kind of case and she is not sure how she feels about it. Samantha definitely feels for Buddy and his family but she is beginning to see just how big and powerful the coal companies are against just a small hardworking miner and his family.

Study Questions

1) Who do Samantha, Donovan and Jeff go to see to help fund the Buddy Ryzer case?

2) How does Marshall explain litigation funding works?

3) How much percentage of the verdict does Marshall think Donovan should take?

4) How much of the percentage of the verdict will the litigation funders take?

5) How is Samantha becoming more like her father by being involved in this case?

Important terms

Putin's frat pack

Cancer cluster

Tort system

Capitalism

Punitive case

Cashmere sweater

Chapter 22

Donovan revels in the enormous victory he had with the Lisa Tate case and everyone shares celebratory drinks together. Donovan does not rest long, however, and he, Jeff and Samantha meet with the Ryzer's to discuss their lawsuit against Lonerock Coal and Casper Slate. The Ryzer's are devastated and furious to find out that the coal company knew for years that Buddy had black lung disease and covered it up.

Then a week later, Donovan files the lawsuit for the Hammer Valley contamination case against Krull mining. In front of a gang of reporters, Donovan claims that Krull Mining has known for years it was poisoning the water supply and covering it up. He also announces that he has the documents to prove it.

Donovan continues to press Samantha to work for him. With these huge lawsuits filed, he was going to need all the help he can get. Samantha is not sure that he likes all the attention from the high profile litigation. He offers her a full time position with a generous salary, but she still declines not sure that she really trusts him.

In a shocking turn of events, four weeks after the Tate victory, and two weeks after filing the Hammer Valley lawsuit, Donovan is found dead - three days before Thanksgiving Day.

Analysis

This chapter recaps the enormous victory of the Tate victory. Using this multimillion-dollar verdict as enormous momentum, Donovan files lawsuits against two of the biggest coal companies and law firms in the country. For the victory roll that Donovan is on and seemingly lead character against the coalmines, it comes as a complete shock that he is found dead.

Study Questions

1) Why does Donovan turn down the $1.5 million settlement offer for the Tate case?

2) How does Buddy react to find out the coal company knew for years he had black lung disease?

3) Whom does Donovan claim owns Krull Mining?

4) How much does the litigation fund want for the two million in funding?

5) Do you think that Donovan's sudden victory and attack mode contributed to his death?

Important Terms

Hometown folks

Cowboy style of lawyering

Egregious

Chapter 23

Donovan's death is announced by Mattie screaming from her office. Jeff has called to say that his plane crashed the night before and his body was found. The entire office is in shock and no one really knows what to say or think. All that is known that air traffic control lost control with his plane and it was found later crashed outside of Charleston.

Plans are made to have the funeral on the Wednesday before Thanksgiving so everyone can move on with their holiday plans. Many of the town folk come by Mattie's with food and condolences. Jeff and Samantha talk privately, and Jeff tells Samantha that he believes that the coal companies killed Donovan. He is convinced that Donovan having the documents that prove the Ryzer case probably has a lot to do with his death. Jeff tells Samantha that there is one document that tells the CEO of Krull Mining that it is cheaper to pay a few lawsuits than pay $80 million to clean up the mess and pollution.

Jeff is deeply depressed over losing his brother who essentially was the only family he had. Samantha listens to him and cannot imagine the grief and heartache he must be feeling. Jeff tells Samantha to start being very careful about what she says and where because they have found bugs in the offices and phones. Samantha can't believe that the coal companies would be doing something like that. She tells Jeff that her father has already begun to look into the plane crash and he will probably be able to help find out exactly what happened.

Analysis

Mattie, the legal aid clinic, and most of the town of Brady are in mourning over the sudden and tragic death of Donovan. Jeff is torn between misery and a desire for revenge believing that his brother was killed over the vendetta he carried for the coal companies. Mattie is too bereft to say much, and Samantha is kind of caught in the middle of the death of someone who was becoming a friend and a conspiracy theory that seems to be snowballing.

Study Questions

1) Who calls Mattie to say that Donovan has died?

2) How did Donovan die?

3) Who is going to help investigate the plane crash?

4) How many incriminating documents does Jeff say Donovan had on the coal companies?

5) Why does Jeff tell Samantha to be careful about where and what she says?

Important Terms

Tort claims

Bugs

Chapter 24

The funeral for Donavan takes place and Mattie speaks eloquently and sadly about her beloved nephew. Samantha sees Judy, Donovan's wife for the first time, and she is a beautiful woman with a small daughter who cries throughout the service. The funeral is very sad and Samantha leaves desiring just to get away from Brady and the coal companies and the Grays and all the drama in Appalachia country. She gets in her car and drives five hours straight to D.C and spends the night with her mother.

The next day, Samantha meets with her father. The litigation funders had pulled the money as soon as they found out Donovan was dead, and her father is trying to put together a legal team that he will essentially coach through the lawsuit. Samantha is tired of talking about it, and doesn't want to think about litigation right now. Marshall is very frank that he doubts Jeff's claims that there was any sabotage, which would essentially mean murder in Donovan's death. He claims that it just doesn't make sense for the companies to take that kind of risk, and he doesn't buy it. Samantha mentions that Donovan had said that he sometimes falls asleep when flying and put the plane on autopilot and maybe something went wrong then.

Samantha tells her dad that she is just really tired over the whole thing and she is not sure that she wants to return. Marshall reminds her that she has real clients, real people who need her and Samantha relinquishes knowing that he is right.

Analysis

Marshall is trying to keep the lawsuits alive that Donovan had started and filed before he died. It is clear that Marshall sees himself in the young exuberant lawyer who went after the big enemies of the little people. It is kind of surprising that Marshall does not believe there was any foul play involved in Donovan's death because it seems just too coincidental to not consider the possibility. Samantha is dragging her feet about returning to Brady, but no doubt she will, as she will feel an obligation to the people who need her.

Study Questions

1) Why does Marshall think Donovan's death was just an accident?

2) Why does the small town usually have an open casket funeral?

3) Where does Samantha take off to after the funeral?

4) What is the NTSB saying about the crash according to Marshall?

5) Why does Samantha not want to go back to Brady?

Important Terms

Open casket

Eulogy

Chapter 25

Samantha has returned to Brady and is greeted at the office by an angry clan that she soon finds are the Crump children. Mrs. Francine Crump's grown children had found out about her intention to leave the family land to a preservation, and they angrily confront Samantha. Annette comes in and helps weather the assault with Samantha. The children insist with a hesitant Mrs. Crump that the will be changed to leave the land in equal parts to them. Annette tells them to leave and come back in a few days for the new will. After they leave, Annette tells Samantha to call Francine and talk to her before changing the will and tell her that to do so will cost $200. Annette and Samantha both know the old lady is being bullied by her children.

Annette and Samantha head court where they find that Randy and Phoebe Fanning are in jail for meth possession. Annette and Samantha talk briefly with Phoebe who is terrified about what is going to happen to her children. Annette tells her that she is facing considerable time in jail. Annette receives a text message that the FBI is raiding Donovan's office and Annette and Samantha leave the courthouse and head to his office. Mattie reads over the search warrant and finds that they are authorized to remove just about everything. Mattie suspects that Krull Mining has put up the US Attorney General filing theft charges over the documents and also using the action as a ploy to scare of possible other future litigators. The FBI also searches Donovan's home, and Mattie tells Annette and Samantha that Jeff wants to have a sit down with them and have a discussion about what to do next.

Analysis

Samantha feels sorry for Mrs. Crump knowing that she is being bullied by her children and is not sure how to handle the changing of the will. Annette feels like probably when Samantha talks to her, she will still not want to leave the land to her children. Samantha sympathizes with the plight that Phoebe is in but wonders why she never thought so much of her children while she was using meth and staying with Randy. Now that the FBI is involved, Samantha is even more wary about what she is getting herself into and how far this litigation against the coal company is going to go - and how much it is going to cost everyone.

Study Questions

1) What excuse do the children say is the reason Mrs. Crump changed her will?

2) What are Randy and Phoebe Fanning arrested for?

3) What is the FBI looking for at Donovan's office and house?

4) What do you think Jeff and Mattie are going to want to do next? Are they going to pick up where Donovan left off or just let the lawsuits go?

Important Terms

Search warrant

Alzheimer's

Legally competent

Bail hearing

Disposition

Chapter 26

Jeff, Mattie, Annette and Samantha all meet in a motel room to discuss the issues surrounding Donovan's death. Samantha realizes they are in the very same room where Pamela Booker and her children had stayed just over a month ago. Samantha listens to the conspiracy theories that Jeff is spinning about the Krull Mining and the FBI and the attorney general and gets very frustrated and leaves. She is tired of hearing about these missing documents that were probably illegally taken and she doesn't want to have any part of it. Additionally, she feels like the breaking down of Donovan's estate is just none of her business and she feels wrong about knowing more about what is happening than Donovan's wife.

While walking the streets after eating by herself at the grill, Samantha is confronted by a man she calls "Bozo" who threatens her by telling her she better watch herself. Bozo tells her that she better stick to her clients at the legal aid clinic and that is it. Samantha stands her ground and threatens to scream and Bozo leaves.

Jeff then meets her near where she is staying and she tells him about her encounter with Bozo. Jeff says that there are two men parked in a black Ford pickup truck watching them right now and one of them is probably the same goon that confronted her. He then tells her that Donovan used various disguises and hid out at Krull Mining for three days and copied the documents. He then put them in garbage bags and posed as an FBI agent to recover them from the landfill. Krull Mining knows they were broken in to but since Donovan used disguises they don't know for sure that it was him. Jeff gives Samantha a prepaid cell phone saying that he is going to be disappearing for a few days, and he wants her to have the phone so he can have someone to talk to.

Analysis

Samantha is reaching the end of her rope with the Donovan drama and walks out on a conspiracy meeting discussing what is going to happen next. Samantha continues to say that she wants nothing to do with any of it, but the others insist including her, especially Jeff. He says that she is the most trustworthy because she is new, doesn't know anyone or anything and is uncorrupted. Samantha reluctantly takes the cell phone, so it seems likely that she is still going to be dragged into the ongoing drama surrounding Donovan and the Krull mining documents.

Study Questions

1) Why does Samantha get upset at the motel room and leave?

2) What happens to Samantha on the street when she goes out for a walk?

3) Why does Jeff want her to have a prepaid cell phone?

4) How did Donovan get the incriminating documents from Krull Mining?

5) Is what Donovan did legal?

Important Terms

Feigned

Fibbies

Sweating blood

Circling like vultures

Chapter 27

Samantha meets with Buddy and Mavis Ryzer at the Cedar Grove Missionary Baptist Church. Samantha explains to them that now that Donovan is dead, the funding has fallen through and no one wants to take case. The only choice they have is to dismiss the case. Buddy is hurt and angry and refuses to sign the papers to dismiss the lawsuit. The Ryzer's do not understand why Samantha will not take it because she is a lawyer, and no amount of explanations helps the Ryzer's to feel any better. Buddy says that the company is retaliating against him for the lawsuit, changing his shifts, and making him work harder assignments. Samantha feels very sorry for their situation but insists that there is nothing that she can do.

Samantha stops at a gas station there and sees the man Bozo there. She decided to ignore him and leaves. She tells Jeff about seeing him again and he says that it is just a scare tactic to remind her that they are always watching. Samantha drives back to the office and receives a call from an Agent Banahan who wants to talk to Jeff. Mattie has him come to the office and tells him that she does not know where he presently is, but any questioning will be done at her office and in her presence. Mattie tries to find out why the FBI wants to talk to Jeff, but she is unable to get any information from the agent about the reason.

Analysis

Samantha seems to be backing off of taking on the lawsuit to help the Ryzer's that Donovan was going to do. Samantha doesn't seem to be able to make up her mind on what kind of lawyer she wants to be. She likes the small work she has done at the clinic but balks at the larger fights that really make the bigger difference. It does seem that despite her effort to back away, the ones involved like Mattie and Jeff are going to keep reeling her back in.

Study Questions

1) Who does Mattie see on her way back from her meeting with the Ryzer's?

2) What is Buddy's reaction to hearing that his case is going to be dismissed?

3) Why has Samantha still not changed Mrs. Crump's will?

4) Why does the FBI want to talk to Jeff?

Important Terms

Paranoia

Fellowship hall

Labored breathing

Jacking around

Paltry sum

Chapter 28

There is another sniper attack by the eco-terrorists against Krull Mining. In all, forty-seven tires were shot out with over $18,000 in damage. The striking difference this time was that guards were present and were in very really danger of being shot and killed. Samantha cannot help but think that Jeff is probably involved with this attack if not the leader. Mattie dismisses this notion as ridiculous.

Mattie and the others at the legal aid clinic decorate the office for Christmas on December 1 and then they all enjoy the town's traditional Christmas parade. Near the end of the parade, Jeff appears next to Samantha and invites her to go hiking with him the next day. He gives her written directions and then disappears into the crowd.

Samantha meets Jeff on Saturday, the next morning, and they travel for a while in a boat and then four- wheel deep into the woods. Samantha realizes that he has taken her to Gray Mountain, and they arrive at the family cabin that she had seen from the air when Donovan had taken her flying.

They hike around a little for the rest of afternoon and then enjoy a dinner at the cabin. Samantha does ask Jeff if he was involved in the eco-terrorist attack at Krull Mining and he denies it. After dinner, they sit by the fire drinking wine and talking. Before long they are kissing and touching and end up having sex before falling asleep.

Then next morning, Jeff takes Samantha to a cave hidden well within what is left of the mountain. Within the cave is a cavern type space filled with the stolen files from Krull Mining. There is also a storage locker of weapons. Samantha is very upset that he brought her there because now she feels like an accessory to a crime. Jeff insists he had no choice because if something happens to him, someone had to know where they were. Samantha is upset, but after returning to the cabin, they have lunch and end up sleeping together again.

Analysis

Samantha suspects that Jeff in involved or even leading the eco-terrorist attacks against Krull Mining despite Mattie's and his denial. She is worried about how deep she is getting involved in some possible criminal activity, but she still ends up sleeping with him. It is evident that Jeff trusts him, but it is hard to determine if this is genuine affection of if he is just possibly manipulating her because she is new and naïve. Samantha is going to be in a very difficult position now if she ends up being questioned by the FBI.

Study Questions

1) Who appears to Samantha at the end of the parade?

2) How is the most recent attack against Krull Mining different than the previous ones?

3) Where does Jeff take Samantha on their Saturday hike?

4) Do you think Jeff genuinely likes Samantha or is he just using her?

5) What is Mattie's reaction to Samantha suggesting that Jeff is involved in the eco-terrorist shooting?

Important Terms

Cavern

Cinder blocks

Chapter 29

Phoebe Fanning's bail is reduced to $1000 and she is able to bond out and be with her children. Samantha warns her, however, that she is no doubt facing five or more years in jail and needs to be prepared for that inevitability and make plans for her kids.

Shortly after talking to Phoebe, Samantha finds out that Mrs. Crump had a massive stroke and is in ICU. She goes over to the hospital and manages to avoid the Crump children. The nurse tells Samantha that the prognosis does not look good, and Samantha dreads the upcoming will issues that are definitely going to come up with her unruly children.

The FBI interviews Jeff at the legal aid office and Mattie acts as his attorney. She advises him to answer their questions precisely, without lying, and to not offer more information than what is asked. Jeff refuses to answer most questions about the hard drives and documents under Mattie's counsel and the agents become frustrated and leave promising to return.

Samantha, Mattie and Jeff then go to court to start the probate over Donovan's will and estate. Jeff tells Mattie and Samantha that the plane crash investigation has determined that the crash was caused by sudden engine failure. Jeff speculates that the B nut that attaches the carburetor to the fuel line was loosened and then came off during vibrations from the flight. This would cause the engine to sputter and then shut down completely very quickly. Jeff claims that it would not be that difficult to tamper with a B nut, but surveillance footage from around the airport the night before does not show anyone around.

Jeff tells Samantha that he is going to be away for a few weeks and casually wishes her a Merry Christmas and Happy New Year. Mrs. Crump dies shortly after being rushed to the hospital and the Crump clan descends on the legal aid office to fight the will. They claim that the will was destroyed by their mother who told them so, and, if that happens to be true, than legally the estate would be equally split among the children. The Crump children are advised to go find an attorney to deal with this new set of facts as neither Annette nor Samantha want to deal with these people any longer. The next day, the will Mrs. Crump had signed arrives in the mail addressed to Samantha.

Analysis

Samantha returns to helping in the small cases that she can make a difference as in Phoebe's case. She listens to the conspiracy theory from Jeff about the B nut, but she remains skeptical and not wanting to think too much about it. The Crump will saga and drama continues and doesn't look like it is going to end soon since now Samantha knows they lied. Mrs. Crump sincerely wanted her land protected and evidently did not trust her children as she mailed her will to Samantha.

Study Questions

1) How much jail time is Phoebe Fanning facing?

2) Who has a massive stroke and dies shortly after?

3) Why do the Crump children say the will was destroyed?

4) What does Jeff think caused the engine failure in Donovan's plane?

5) What arrives in the mail that promises more troubles for Samantha?

Important Terms

B nut

Carburetor

Blood relatives

Torrent of abuse

Chapter 30

Samantha goes back to New York for Christmas and her mother joins her there for the third year in a row. She had lunch with her old flame Henry but they both realize they have nothing in common anymore and part ways. A couple of days after Christmas, Jeff calls her and asks to see her because he just happens to be in the city.

They meet and Jeff tells her that he has been talking with a high-powered lawyer named Jarrett London who had been close with Donovan. Samantha is furious to hear that London wants to meet with her as well to discuss the documents and accuses Jeff of sucking her into something she wants nothing to do with. She nevertheless agrees to meet London and listen to what he has to say. The tension worsens when London reveals what he really wants is Samantha's mother at justice to say something to the US Attorney general about having the FBI back off. Samantha again states she wants nothing to do with this conspiracy theory and angrily leaves.

Jeff claims to Samantha that he really did not know London was going to ask about her mother's pull at justice, and Samantha sulkily agrees to dinner. During dinner, Jeff asks Samantha to take over Donovan's practice, at least for the next eighteen months and close out some of the open cases that Donovan left behind. Samantha lists many reasons why she has no interest in staying in Brady, and Jeff tries relentlessly to persuade her. Samantha agrees to stay for the short term, but that is it because Brady is just not her world.

Analysis

Despite Samantha still saying she doesn't want to be part of the case, she still meets with Jeff and London. It does seem like Jeff has ulterior motives beyond personal, especially when Samantha is asked to approach her mother at justice for a favor. Samantha seems much happier when she is back in the city, but she feels obligated to complete her year internship even though it is getting her involved in something much darker than she has ever experienced or cared to.

Study Questions

1) Where does Samantha spend Christmas and who joins her?

2) Why is Samantha happier back in the New York City?

3) What does Jarrett London want Samantha to ask her mother?

 4) Why does Samantha keep seeing Jeff if she suspects that he is trouble?

Important Terms

Drinking port

Tomcat

Crostini

Lobbyist

Chapter 31

Samantha goes to court with Pamela Booker over her wage garnishment case. A sympathetic judge awards her $1300 for lost wages and an additional $10,000 in damages. Samantha is elated over the win at her fist court hearing, but Mattie cautions her against being too happy until the check actually arrives.

News arrives that Jeff was arrested at an airport in Charleston for trespassing. He calls Samantha after he is bailed out and tells her that he had been investigating. He said that he was able to gain access to the planes and actually sit in one for about ten minutes completely unnoticed because of the lax security. Jeff allowed himself to be noticed by a guard who was pleasant and talkative. Jeff used a cover story that he was just a pilot that wanted to see the planes up closer. The guard really didn't have much of a problem with him, but was obliged to do his job anyway. Jeff finds out that a security guard that was working when Donovan took off on his last flight is not working there anymore and he plans on tracking him down.

Samantha accompanies Mattie to court over a black lung disease case that has been dragging on for over thirteen years. Wally Landry was fifty-eight years old, required oxygen to breathe and confined to a wheelchair. As the usual case went, he had been awarded benefits but then had been caught up in an appeal for years and had not seen any money. Mattie and Samantha are approached by the defense counsel, Trent Fuller, who now is also assigned the Buddy Ryzer case. Trent openly threatens Samantha by saying that he will sue her for libel and she better back off. Samantha is shocked at the brazenness of this lawyer and thinks about how she would never be talked to or treated like this back at her old law firm.

Analysis

Jeff is continuing to investigate his brother's death as sabotage or murder. He needs to find the security guard who doesn't work there anymore and this guard might have some pertinent information. Samantha knows that even with being arrested, Jeff is not going to stop his investigation until he finds out the truth. Samantha is exhilarated at her first experience in court. She imagines she feels the same thrill as Donovan felt over his verdict. Being threatened later that day in court by Trent Fuller anger and frustrates her. She can't believe that another lawyer actually threatened her and she again thinks about the city and misses her life there.

Study Questions

1) What is the judge's decision in the Pamela Booker hearing?

2) What was Jeff doing when he was arrested?

3) Why does Trent Fuller threaten Samantha in court?

4) Why has the Wally Landry case been dragging on for over thirteen years?

Important terms

Misdemeanor

Office contingencies

Looming mess

Swaggered

Chapter 32

Samantha receives an email from Jarrett London requesting that they meet. He discreetly states that he needs the documents and also says that there has been no word from their friends in Washington, which, is a reference to her mother. Samantha had briefly told her mother a general outline of the case, but had not directly asked her to say anything about it. Samantha's mother was not really interested in the details anyway, and Samantha chose not to pursue the matter with her.

Andy Grubman, Samantha's old boss, emails her and offers her a job at a new firm he is starting. He tells that he has had enough of big law and wants to start up a little boutique style law firm with about twenty associates. He already has a couple of clients lined up, and promises fifty-hour workweek and the same kind of compensation and benefits she received before. Samantha is caught off guard by this offer and decided she needs some time to think about it. She writes a rough draft reply asking for some more details but doesn't send it.

Jeff shows up that evening at her apartment and fills her in on his airport investigation. He found out that the night before Donovan's flight a plane landed and one passenger stayed on board overnight. Jeff found the guard, Brad that was working that night and found all this out from him. Jeff says the plane belonged to a charter company hired by coal companies and he is going to find out more about the plane and who chartered it as soon as he can.

Analysis

Samantha has decisions to make sooner than she expected to about her future. While it makes sense for her to take Andy up on his offer, she is not sure that she can just up and leave Mattie with all the cases she is involved in and helping with. Samantha is only three months in to her year internship, and really can't figure out what direction to go in. Jeff is making some progress in his private investigation into Donovan's death and suspicious activity is starting to suggest that foul play may have been involved.

Study Questions

1) Why is Jarrett London anxious to get the Krull Mining documents?

2) What offer does Andy Grubman make Samantha?

3) What do you think Samantha is going to decide about the boutique law firm?

4) What does Jeff find out about the night at the airport before Donovan's flight?

5) Do you think Donovan's plane was sabotaged or was it just a freak accident?

Important Terms

Boutique

Complicity

Demeaning ambush

Nuisance action

Billable hours

Chapter 33

When Samantha wakes up Jeff is gone and she doesn't know what time he slipped away. She arrives first at the clinic, makes coffee and thinks some more about Andy's offer. Mattie arrives and said that they need to find out if the Crumps have gone to any other lawyers about their mother's will. Samantha finds talks to Lee Chatham and finds out that yes the Crumps had retained him to fight the will. Samantha then tells him that his clients are lying to him and faxes him a copy of the actual will that was not destroyed but mailed to the clinic.

Samantha gets a friendly reply from Andy to an email she had sent requesting more details and dictating some terms. Basically, Andy agrees with everything she wants and Samantha decides that she is probably going to accept. Jeff calls as well and invites her to the cabin on Saturday, but she says that she will let him know later.

Later that morning, Buddy and Mavis Ryzer show up in tears at the clinic to see Samantha. Buddy tells her that he was fired that morning from the coal company, and now they have nothing and do not know what to do. Buddy is having a terrible time breathing, and Samantha feels immensely sorry for them. She reminds them that these cases drag on for years, and Buddy sadly laments he probably won't live long enough to see it through. The Ryzer's beg her to take the appeal lawsuit and sincerely thank her for being the only lawyer they have ever had, and really the only person, who has tried to help them.

Analysis

Samantha is leaning towards taking Andy up on his offer and leaving the coal company and poor legal aid drama in Brady behind. She is torn between fulfilling her commitment to the year internship to Mattie, and just making a decision to move on with her life. She is growing apart from Jeff and is distancing herself both from his advances and the investigation he is pursuing. Samantha feels very badly for the Ryzer's but just does not feel that she is neither up for the job of years of litigation nor want to make that kind of commitment.

Study Questions

1) What does Samantha do in the mornings at the legal aid clinic she would never do at a real law firm?

2) Why does Samantha tell the Crump's new lawyer about the actual will that was mailed to the clinic before Mrs. Crump died?

3) Why did Buddy get fired from the coal company and what are their options now?

4) Is Samantha going to stay and help the Ryzer's or will she take Andy's offer and go work for him?

Important Terms

Gagging fit

Christian-like to hate

No golden parachute

Wintertime blues

Chapter 34

Samantha takes Jeff up on his offer to go hiking and to the cabin. When she meets him at the truck, she notices two kayaks and three backpacks loaded in the back. Samantha reminds him that she is from the city and has never been kayaking before. Jeff replies that he is not worried about it because the water is probably going to be too low anyway.

The water is too low at the stream so they spend most of the day hiking around Gray Mountain. Jeff grills some steaks and they enjoy a nice dinner and some wine by the fire. Samantha awakens around four in the morning to find that she is alone in the cabin and two of the backpacks are missing. She realizes that Jeff had used her and the kayaks as a ruse to throw off whoever was following them and was now filling up the backpacks with the Krull Mining documents. Samantha hears Jeff come back inside, but pretends to be asleep and eventually drifts away.

Analysis

Jeff is taking full advantage of Samantha's "sex with no strings" arrangement and is using her as cover. It doesn't seem to bother him that he is both incriminating her and putting her in danger. Samantha is showing poor judgment by not confronting Jeff and completely distancing herself from him.

Study Questions

1) Why does Samantha not know what kayaks are when she sees them?

2) Did Jeff ever really intend to kayak that day?

3) Why does Jeff disappear in the middle of the night?

4) Why does Samantha pretend to be asleep when Jeff returns?

5) What does Samantha suspect Jeff was doing when he left her alone in the cabin?

Important Terms

Kayak

Sex with no strings

Merlot

Chapter 35

Samantha receives and email from her old colleague Izabelle regarding Andy's offer. Izabelle was offered the same job, but she is really enjoying her internship helping children convicted as adults. Like Samantha, Izabelle is unsure if she wants to jump right back into virtually the same meaningless rat race that she got away from. Izabelle also dispel some of the perks and facts that Andy had grazed over and the job offer does not sound as great anymore to Samantha as it did initially.

The check for $11,300 arrives for Pamela Booker and Samantha drives it over to the lamp factory and presents it to a shocked and overwhelmed Pamela. Samantha gives her some pro bono financial advice and drives back to the clinic thrilled and proud of herself for winning her first case and accomplishing something that truly helped someone in need.

Mattie receives and an anonymous phone call that the clinic is to be raided in thirty minutes by the FBI. They send the laptops with Barb away from the office planning to say they were going to the technicians to fix some glitches. Files are hurriedly backed up on flash drives and these are taken and hidden at the local law library. Mattie retains Hump as their criminal attorney and he happily agrees to come over.

The FBI barges in shortly after and Agent Frohmeyer and Banahan present Mattie with a search warrant to retrieve all files, documents etc. relating to the law offices of Donovan Gray. Annette threatens to bring a lawsuit if they touch her files that have nothing to do with Donovan anyway. The FBI decides to start with Samantha's office, and Hump asks to talk with the agents. After the raid, Mattie ask Samantha to come over for dinner saying they need to talk.

Analysis

Samantha finds out the job offer from Andy is not really as great as he made it sound, and Izabelle talking about the job reminds Samantha of all the things she really disliked about her former life. Her relationship with Jeff has brought the FBI down on the clinic. Mattie suspects Samantha knows more about what is going on then she is letting on.

Study Questions

1) What are some of the drawbacks to Andy's job offer that Izabelle tells Samantha about?

2) What surprise arrives in the mail for Samantha?

3) What does Samantha advise Pamela to do with the money?

4) Who do you think was the anonymous tipper who called Mattie?

5) Why does the FBI want Samantha's files in particular?

Important Terms

Halitosis

Pro bono

Flash drives

Ominous

Chapter 36

→ Buddy Ryzer drives to a scenic overlook and commits suicide. Samantha is devastated by the news and drives over to Mattie's to talk. She asks for a personal day or two feeling overwhelmed by all the deaths and tragedies and FBI raids.

→ Samantha drives to Charlottesville and meets both her parents at a local hotel bar. This is the first time that her parents have been together in over eleven years. Samantha is tired and overwhelmed and desperately needs to talk to her parents, tell them everything that has happened, and get their advice. Both listen patiently and respectively as Samantha relays the events of the past few months. Predictably, Marshall thinks that Samantha should avoid the job with Andy, and Karen thinks Samantha should get out of Brady and the drama. Both agree that Samantha needs to distance herself from Jeff and absolutely have nothing more to do with the stolen documents from Krull Mining. Karen says that she will try and get the FBI to back off but says that she does not have much pull there, which Marshall silently disbelieves.

Analysis

With the suicide of Buddy, Samantha has had about all the grief and drama that she can handle. She leaves Brady for a couple of personal days and meets with her parents. This is probably the smartest decision that Samantha has made since all the trouble began in Brady. Both her parents are smart and powerful, and have Samantha's best interest at heart. Although neither can offer a clear direction that Samantha should take, they mutually offer sound advice, and help Samantha unburden herself from the problems in Brady.

Study Questions

1) What happens to Buddy Ryzer and why?

2) Who does Samantha meet in Charlottesville for advice?

3) What do Marshall and Karen think Samantha should do?

4) Why does Samantha tear up when she sees her parents together?

Important Terms

Spiffed up version of corporate law

White-collar guys

Therapeutic

Rifled through

Chapter 37

Samantha meets Jeff for lunch in Roanoke. She tells him that she had spoken to both her parents about everything. Jeff asks if her mother is going to help with the FBI, and Samantha says that her mother will but she does not know what the results will be.

Samantha confronts Jeff about the evening he disappeared in the middle of the night at the cabin, and tells him she knows exactly what he is using for. Jeff does not deny it, and says that he needs her for cover while he gets the documents. Jeff then asks Samantha point blank to deliver the documents to London because it is just too risky for him to do it. Samantha balks and Jeff insists that he needs her help, and she just must help him because so much is at stake.

Later, when Samantha returns to the office, she finds that her computer has been returned and she thinks maybe her mother has more friends and power than originally thought.

Analysis

Samantha finally confronts Jeff about the real reason that he is seeing her. Somewhat nobly, Jeff does not deny that he is using her for cover while he retrieves the documents. Not really caring for the risk that he is asking her to take, Jeff pleads with Samantha to deliver the documents to London. It also seems that Samantha has underestimated the power her mother has at justice when Samantha returns to the clinic to find her computer returned from the FBI.

Study Questions

1) Why does Samantha decide to confront Jeff about leaving in the middle of the night at the cabin?

2) What does Jeff ask Samantha to do?

3) What are the ramifications if Samantha gets caught with the Krull Mining documents?

4) Why is Samantha surprised to see her computer back on her desk when she returns to the clinic?

Important Terms

Unlimited muscle

Getting grilled

Lovebirds

Chapter 38

Samantha receives another email from Andy regarding the job offer. He says they cannot wait until Sept 1 for her to start because things are already getting busy. He offers $150,000 with three weeks of paid vacation along with all the usual perks. Although she will not have to start until May 1, he still wants an answer by the end of the month.

The funeral for Buddy Ryzer takes place and it is a long and depressing affair. Hundreds of people show up to show their respects, to gossip, and as Mattie says, enjoy the food as well. Samantha and Mattie try to slip away after the service, but Mavis sees Samantha and asks her to please stay for the dinner. Mattie and Samantha sit with Mavis and some of the family. Keely, the Ryzer's thirteen-year-old daughter, edges over next to Samantha and asks to hold her hand. Keely tells Samantha that her daddy liked Samantha very much and asks her to please stay and help them. Samantha tries to gently tell Keely that there are other lawyers, but Keely is adamant saying that her daddy said Samantha was the only lawyer that would help them.

Analysis

Andy is still trying hard to recruit Samantha to come and work for him at his new firm. It almost seems like Samantha could dictate her own terms and Andy would agree. The funeral for Buddy Ryzer is a sad affair. To make Samantha's decision even harder, Keely pleads with Samantha to help them. Samantha is going to have to decide to follow her heart or her head in which direction she chooses.

Study Questions

1) What are the terms of the job offer Andy proposes to Samantha?

2) What are some of the reasons Mattie says rural funerals are so large?

3) Why does Samantha stay after the service instead of leaving like she wanted to?

4) What does Keely tell Samantha about what her daddy told her?

Important Terms

Baptist potluck

Mourners

Pallbearers

Closed casket

Chapter 39

Samantha and Jeff take off back to the cabin and spend the day kayaking and hiking. That night, Jeff leaves Samantha at the cabin while he goes to the cave to retrieve the rest of the documents. Samantha hears gunshots and Jeff comes running back. He tells her that the goons had followed him and shot at him. He had fired back and shot one in the leg. Samantha is mortified that he shot someone, but Jeff shrugs it off. He leaves Samantha a Glock and strict instructions to not leave the cabin and protect the documents while he goes back to get the last load.

Shortly after he leaves again, Samantha hears more gunfire and a scream. Thinking that it might be Jeff, she runs out into the night leaving the gun and the documents. Samantha soon realizes this is kind of foolish, running around blindly in the night, and returns to the cabin. To her horror, she finds the documents that were in coolers are gone along with the gun. Jeff returns again with the rest of the documents and she tells him what happened. He says they have to leave now, and when they get back to the jeep, Vic is there and he has the coolers. Jeff tells Samantha he had Vic along for backup and now they needed to get the documents to London.

They meet London at his private jet and deliver all of the Krull Mining documents. London tells Samantha that he knows that she has lots of options, but he really could use her help on this case. He also mentions that the FBI has backed off completely and thinks they do have friends in Washington after all, to which Samantha just smiles.

Analysis

Samantha spends another day with Jeff out at Gray Mountain knowing that night; he is going to get the rest of the documents against Krull Mining that Donovan had stashed away. She manages to keep her curiosity in check and does not look at any of them while she is left on guard at the cabin. Jeff clearly does not trust her too much because he did not tell her that Vic was in on this with them and was being his backup. London now has the documents, and Samantha hopes that she can close this chapter of her life and move on.

Study Questions

1) Who does Jeff shoot in the woods?

2) Why does Samantha leave the cabin and the documents inside?

3) Who took the coolers and the gun while Samantha was in the woods?
Vic

4) What is London going to do now that he has all in the incriminating evidence against Krull Mining?

5) What offer does London make to Samantha?

Important Terms

Goons

Loot

Hibernating

Chapter 40

Samantha meets with Mattie on Monday morning and tells her everything that happened over the weekend with Jeff and the cabin and the Krull Mining documents. Mattie is as relived as Samantha that particular chapter of their life is over.

Jeff calls and asks Samantha to meet him over at Donovan's office. He tells her that he is leaving for a few months. He says he thinks he knows who killed Donovan, but Samantha does not want to hear or talk about it. Jeff asks her if she will still be around when he gets back and Samantha says she doesn't know. Samantha tells him that she does not belong in Brady, and she does not want him to think about her anyway. She allows him to give her a kiss goodbye and they part ways.

Back at the office, Samantha has yet another email from Andy. He has raised the offer and thrown in more perks. Samantha prints off the email and goes to talk to Mattie. Samantha shows Mattie the email, and Mattie is impressed. Samantha then says that she has made her decision. She wants to handle the Tate case and see what she can do to help the Ryzer's as well. She can't stay on as an unpaid intern, but she has decided she does have a taste and natural flair for litigation and wants to put her lawyering skills to good use. Mattie is thrilled to bring her on board and they agree on terms. Samantha with great satisfaction, tears up the email from Andy, and leaves Mattie's office.

Analysis

Samantha brings Mattie up to speed on everything that she has been involved in with Jeff, and the transferring of the Krull Mining documents to London. It is doubtful that will be the last that Samantha hears about any of that, but for now she feels like she can move on from the Gray drama and tragedy.

After email from Andy outlining the life that he is offering compels Samantha to choose to stay in Brady and help the people that truly help her. Mattie believes deeply in Samantha and reaches in to the clinic's funds to change Samantha's status from an unpaid intern to a paid associate. The internship changed Samantha in ways that she never would have imagined, and now begins a new chapter of life as a different kind of lawyer.

Study Questions

1) What does Jeff tell Samantha at Donovan's office?

2) What is the latest offer Andy makes to Samantha?

3) What terms to Mattie and Samantha agree to?

4) What does Samantha want to do with her remaining time at the clinic?

Critical Reviews

The Washington Post wrote that John Grisham did a "justice to the physical beauty of Appalachia and to the decency of most of its people" even though his subject mostly revolved around the real suffering inflicted on those that work for the coal mining companies who are protected both by big law firms and big politics.

Anderson, Patrick. (2014, October 19). Book Review: John Grisham's 'Gray Mountain is a searing look at Big Coal. *The Washington Post.* Retrieved from http://www.washingtonpost.com

USA Today gave 4.5 stars stating that if this novel does not convince you that John Grisham does not have strong opinions about the inequities of the legal system than nothing will. *Gray Mountain* is different from his other novels in that it is not so much a legal thriller but a bold political statement and defense of social advocacy. The sad story of the dying coal miners leaves the reader sensitive to their plight and a desire to see action taken.

Moore, Dennis. (2014, October 20). John Grisham climbs the summit in 'Gray Mountain.' *USA Today.*   Retrieved from http://www.usatoday.com.

Publisher's Weekly reviewed *Gray Mountain* as a "tepid legal thriller" that may be the start of a character series for him. The book does end somewhat open-ended with the coal mining cases that Samantha takes on. Grisham passionately captures the suffering life of the coal miners and their families, but the usual big characters and legal thrills are very much absent in this latest Grisham novel.

Gray Mountain will keep you up all night. Grisham commits his finest writing in this novel and weaves a tale with "vigor, detail, dazzling complexity and just plain good reading."

Moul, Francis. (2014, November 25). Review: 'Gray Mountain' by John Grisham. *Journal Star*. Retrieved from http://journalstar.com

Final Thoughts

I thought this was a very weak John Grisham book. Halfway into the book, I was still waiting for something to happen and know exactly what the main focus was going to be. Killing off a main character was the only eyebrow raising part of the book, and even then that was not developed into anything really that interesting. Grisham's main character Samantha is so indecisive that it is really frustrating. Her going back and forth on wanting to go back to New York City or stay in Brady is so incessant it gets ridiculous, and eventually the reader just doesn't even care what she does. Grisham had a very meaningful story and social issue presented that could have been very powerful, but he definitely failed with his final product.

Glossary

Appalachia - a rural region of the southeast United States

Bar exam - an exam that must be passed to become a licensed attorney

Big Law - rich powerful law firms that have hundreds of lawyers and clients

Black lung disease - a disease of the lungs from inhaling coal dust

Bureaucrat - an official who works by fixed routine with exercising judgment

Claustrophobic - to be afraid of small spaces

Coal Sludge - the by-product of washing mine coal; very toxic to people and the environment

Deadbeat - someone who provides no use or purpose to people or society

Debtor's prison - an outlawed practice in which people who owed money were imprisoned until they could pay their debt

Disbarred - an attorney who has lost his license to practice law

Discernible - able to be perceived by a sense or the mind

Donovan Gray - renegade attorney determined to sue and bring down big coal companies

Equal Protection Clause of the Fourteenth Amendment - no state shall deny any person equal rights under the law

Exxon Valdez - an oil tanker that ran aground in 1989 spilling thousands of gallons of oil into the Alaskan waters

Fannie Mae - a financial lending company

Foundation money - money that is set-aside for a certain stated purpose

Garage apartment - a space over a separate garage that has been renovated and made livable

Goons - slang for bad guys

Hybrid - containing mixed elements

Hillbilly - slang term for someone born and lives in the country

Incriminating -something that suggests one is guilty of something

Injunction - a ruling to stop an action

Jeff Gray - Donovan's brother

Jihadists - an Islamist who fights for the fundamentals of Islam to be the rule

Karen Kofer - Samantha's mother; a powerful attorney with the Justice department

Leukemia - a cancer that affects the blood

Loot - treasure

Litigation - an action brought in court to enforce a right

Litigation funders - investors that fund large lawsuits for a percentage of the award

Lobbyist - a person who raises support for a cause

Malicious wounding - an assault that intended serious harm usually with a weapon

Marshall Kofer - Samantha's father; a disbarred lawyer who spent time in jail for corruption

Mattie Wyatt - lawyer who owns Mountain Aid Legal Clinic; Donovan's aunt

Mediation - to serve as middleman or go between; to help reach an agreement

Meth - a potent recreational drug

Punitive damages - a financial award that is supposed to offset financial or emotional suffering

Quaint - different or unique

Recession - an economic depression

Samantha - a lawyer from New York City who spend a year internship in Brady, Virginia at a nonprofit

Sassafras - a type of tree; slang for someone who has amused or sassed you

Shell Company - a nonexistent company used to hide money usually for tax purposes

Slurry - a mixture of chemicals and coal sludge

Strip-mining - the process of mining from coal by razing everything on the land layer by layer

Toxic waste - dangerous and poisonous by-products of washing coal

Recommended Reading:

The Firm - John Grisham's first bestseller and movie starring Tom Cruise

A Time To Kill - the first Grisham novel about a father on trial for killing the men who raped his daughter

Sycamore Row - a return to the setting of A Time to Kill bringing back one of Grisham's most popular lawyers every created - Jeff Brigance.

19240184R00059

Made in the USA
Middletown, DE
10 April 2015